One to Ten
and
Back Again

For

1. Millie

2. Rosie   6. Ina

3. Isabel   7. Ettie

4. Gabriel   8. Mairi

5. Jim   9. Carina

                10. Thomas

From Nick and Sue

PUFFIN BOOKS

Published by the Penguin Group
Penguin Books Ltd, 80 Strand, London WC2R 0RL, England
Penguin Group (USA), Inc., 375 Hudson Street, New York, New York 10014, USA
Penguin Books Australia Ltd, 250 Camberwell Road, Camberwell, Victoria 3124, Australia
Penguin Books Canada Ltd, 10 Alcorn Avenue, Toronto, Ontario, Canada M4V 3B2
Penguin Books India (P) Ltd, 11 Community Centre, Panchsheel Park, New Delhi – 110 017, India
Penguin Group (NZ), cnr Airborne and Rosedale Roads, Albany, Auckland 1310, New Zealand
Penguin Books (South Africa) (Pty) Ltd, 24 Sturdee Avenue, Rosebank 2196, South Africa

Penguin Books Ltd, Registered Offices: 80 Strand, London WC2R 0RL, England

www.penguin.com

First published in hardback 2004
Published in paperback 2005
10 9 8 7 6 5 4

Text and illustrations copyright © Sue Heap and Nick Sharratt, 2004
All rights reserved

The moral right of the authors and illustrators has been asserted

Manufactured in China

British Library Cataloguing in Publication Data
A CIP catalogue record for this book is available from the British Library

ISBN-13: 978-0-14056-786-1
ISBN-10: 0-14056-786-0

One to Ten and Back Again

Sue Heap and Nick Sharratt

PUFFIN

One boy called Nick,

One girl called Sue,

Two woolly gloves,

Two shiny shoes.

Three round buttons,

Four bright bows,

Five pink pigs,

Six sheep in a row.

Seven bobbing boats,

Eight fish in the sea,

Nine chocolate biscuits

and ten cakes for tea.

Ten oranges,

Nine lemons,

Eight crayons,

Seven pens,

Six butterflies,

Five bumble bees,

Four ducks

and three red hens.

Two elephants,

Two crocodiles,

One Sue, one Nick,

One yellow moon,

a hundred stars,

that's how the story ends!

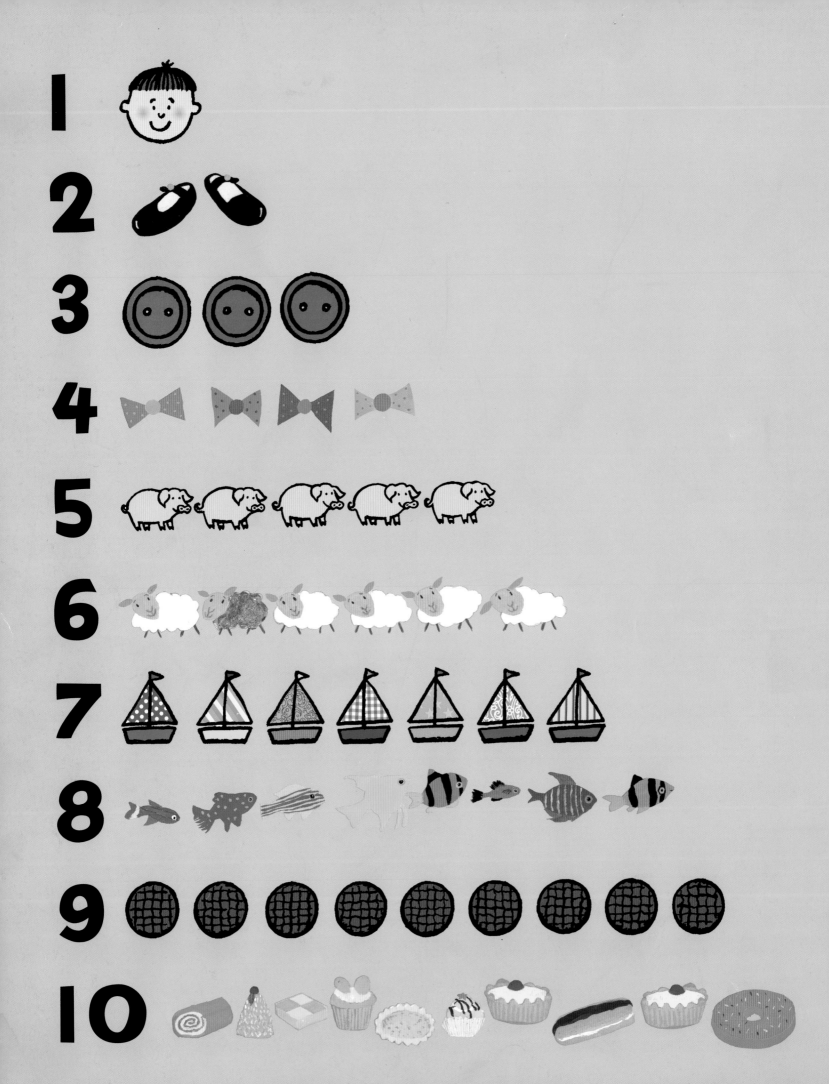

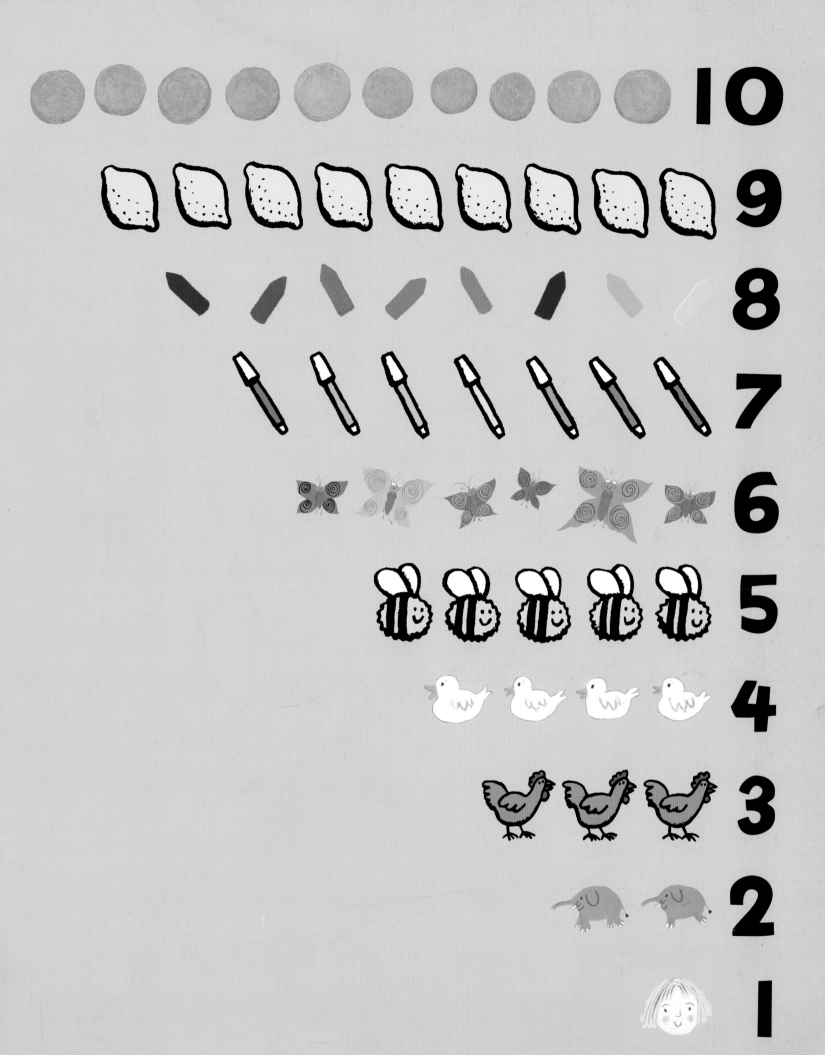

Goodbye, Nick!
Goodbye, Sue!